nickelodeon

Apples Everywhere!

Adapted by Mickie Matheis

Based on the teleplay "If Timmy Gives You Apples"
by Rachel Vine

Illustrated by Francesco Legramandi and Giulia Priori

A GOLDEN BOOK • NEW YORK

 Published in the United States by Golden Books, an imprint of Random House Children's Books, a division of Penguin Random House LLC, 1745 Broadway, New York, NY 10019, and in Canada by Penguin Random House Canada Limited, Toronto. Golden Books, A Golden Book, A Little Golden Book, the G colophon, and the distinctive gold spine are registered trademarks of Penguin Random House LLC. Nickelodeon, Nick Jr., Sunny Day, and all related titles, logos, and characters are trademarks of Viacom International Inc.
T#: 564006
ISBN 978-0-525-57754-6
rhcbooks.com
Printed in the United States of America
10 9 8 7 6 5 4 3 2 1

One morning at Sunny's Salon, the phone rang. It was Timmy calling from his apple orchard to say he would be late for his haircut. He had been picking apples when his ladder fell over. Now he couldn't get down!

"I'm kind of stuck at the moment," he said. "And I mean *really* stuck—up a tree!"

"We'll be right there!"
Sunny said. "Don't move!"

Sunny and her best friends, Blair and Rox, jumped into the Glam Van and headed for Timmy's orchard.

His ladder had broken when it fell, so Sunny, Blair, and Rox tied together some hairnets to make a big safety net to catch Timmy!

Timmy was back on the ground in no time.

"Thanks so much! What can I do to repay you?" he asked.

“You don’t have to repay us, Timmy,” Sunny replied. “Friends help each other.”

But Timmy wanted to do something nice for Sunny, Rox, and Blair. He gave them a bushel of apples.

Back at the salon, the girls enjoyed the tasty fruit. They had nearly finished the apples when Timmy brought another two bushels.

"And there's plenty more where those came from!" he said. "Happy crunching!"

The next morning, Timmy delivered more apples. And more the day after that, and the day after that, and the day after that!

“The salon’s turned into a giant fruit stand!” Blair exclaimed. Customers couldn’t even get inside. Blair and Rox wanted to tell Timmy to stop bringing apples.

“But it makes him so happy to give them to us,” Sunny said. She couldn’t hurt Timmy’s feelings.

Rox had an idea. They could take the apples back to the orchard! The friends stuffed the apples into the Glam Van, but as soon as Sunny started to drive, the fruit spilled out the back. There were just too many apples, so they took them back to the salon.

When Timmy finally came for his haircut, the salon was so full of apples, they couldn't open the door! Sunny had to work in the Glam Van.

"I had no idea I'd brought you so many apples," Timmy said.

After Sunny cut Timmy's hair, she turned on the hair dryer. Suddenly, the van smelled like apple pie! Some of the apples had gotten stuck in the dryer.

The delicious smell gave Sunny an idea. "We'll hold an apple festival, right here at the salon, and invite the whole town!"

The friends made applesauce, apple butter, apple juice, and apple pie. There were apple-themed games, decorations, and music.

Sunny even styled her hair in a super-sweet apple updo.

"This is one for the Style Files," she said.

Thanks to Timmy's delicious apples, everyone had a wonderful time at the first-ever Friendly Falls Apple Festival.

“We couldn’t have done any of this without your apples!” Sunny told Timmy.

“When life hands you apples,” she said, “make apple pie!”